Copyright © 2020

make believe ideas ltd

The Wilderness, Berkhamsted, Hertfordshire, HP4 2AZ, UK.
501 Nelson Place, P.O. Box 141000, Nashville, TN 37214-1000, USA.

www.makebelieveideas.com
Written by Rosie Greening.
Illustrated by Lara Ede.

Hope the RAINBOW Fairy

Concept by Holly Lansley ∗ Created and Designed by Jane Horne
Written by Rosie Greening ∗ Illustrated by Lara Ede

make
believe
ideas

Hope the RAINBOW Fairy

worked her magic day and night

to spread nice rainbow colors and make Fairyland look bright!

 **Yellow** for the sunshine

and **green** for every tree,

then a hundred other **colors** only fairy eyes can see.

But then one year, a fairy flu
began to slowly spread.
"We need a plan to beat this!"
all the **sneezing** fairies said.

AH-CHOO!

Soon enough, Hope heard the news
of what they had to do . . .

EVERYONE MUST STAY AT HOME TO KEEP SAFE FROM THIS FLU!

So every fairy, young and old,
stayed tucked up in their house,

and quickly, all of Fairyland
was **quiet** as a mouse.

But Hope began to worry.
The fairies needed cheer,
and it seemed the trees and flowers
would be COLORLESS this year!

She opened her computer,

then she called her friends and said:

"There won't be any COLORS if I stay at home instead!"

Hope's friends said, "Don't worry, everyone will understand." But Hope knew that she had to try and **help out** Fairyland.

So Hope began to brainstorm ways
to spread **JOY** from her home,
and help the magic fairies
feel a little less alone.

She sent out **rainbow** popsicles
for everyone to eat,

but they melted in the mail
and left big puddles in the street.

She set up lots of online games for everyone to play,
but the Wi-Fly soon cut out, and it confused Gran anyway!

Finally, Hope waved her wand
to wish the flu away.
But she didn't have the power:
fairy flu was here to **stay!**

"This is bad," cried Fairy Hope.
"I can't fix the flu,

but I can't spread COLOR either,
so what's left for me to do?"

Hope flew sadly to the roof.
"I MISS MY FRIENDS," she said.
Then, as she gazed at Fairyland,
a plan came to her head . . .

She whooshed her wand above her and, as quickly as could be, a **rainbow** shone above her house for everyone to see!

One by one, the fairies saw the **rainbow** far away.
The **colors** made them **hopeful** when so much felt sad and gray.

So the fairies got to work to make big
rainbows of their own.

It made them feel much better
as they knew they weren't alone.

Soon each house in Fairyland
had **rainbows** shining bright.
Each time the fairies saw them,
they knew things would be all right.

And Hope was thrilled that Fairyland had more COLOR than ever.
The fairies were connected:
safe at home, but still together.

THANK YOU

The weeks went by in Fairyland,
until Hope heard one day . . .

THE FAIRY FLU
IS OVER—YOU
CAN MEET AGAIN
AND PLAY!

Hope flew from her house
and all the fairies gave a cheer.
They told her they were grateful
for the joy she'd brought that year.

So even when the world seems gray,
there's color we can share.

With kindness and community,

hope is always there.